TOGETHER

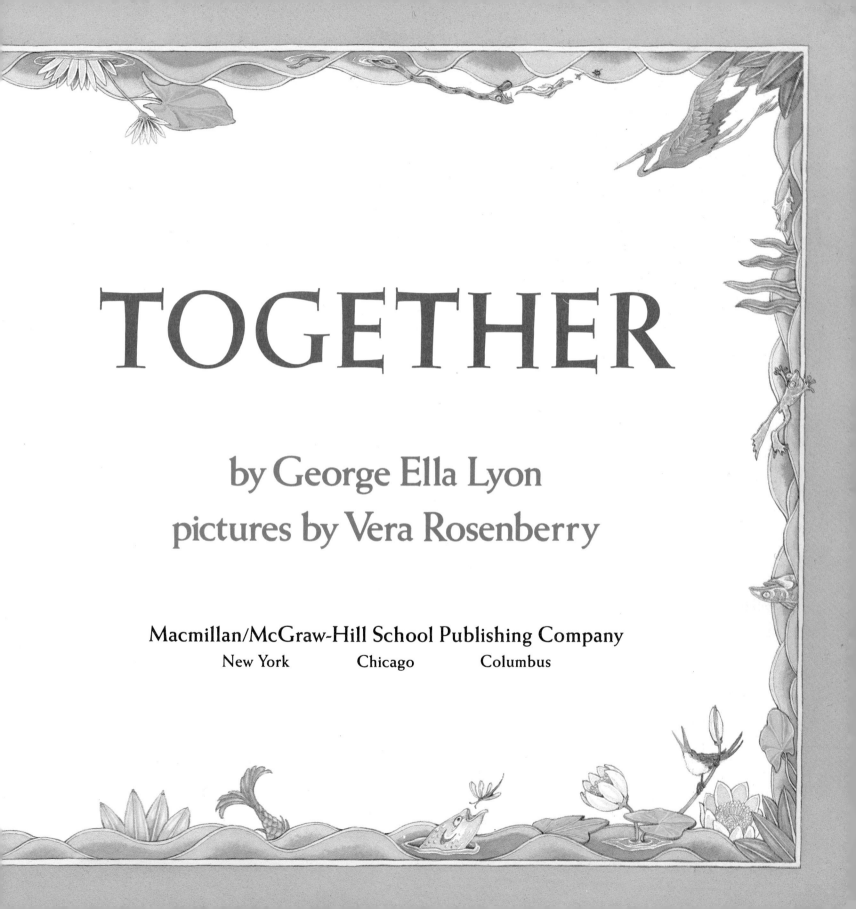

TOGETHER

by George Ella Lyon
pictures by Vera Rosenberry

Macmillan/McGraw-Hill School Publishing Company
New York   Chicago   Columbus

For information regarding permission, write to Orchard Books,
387 Park Avenue South, New York, NY 10016.

This edition is reprinted by permission fo Orchard Books,
a division of Franklin Watts, Inc.

Book design by Mina Greenstein.
The illustrations are watercolor and ink line, done by brush,
and reproduced in full color.

Macmillan/McGraw-Hill School Division.
10 Union Square East
New York, New York 10003

Printed in the United States of America

ISBN 0-02-179095-7 / 1, L. 1

2 3 4 5 6 7 8 9   FED   99 98 97 96 95 94 93 92

For Ben
who gave me the refrain
for Joey
newest joy
for Steve
and seventeen years
together

G.E.L.

For Tanya and Julie

V.R.

You cut the timber
and I'll build the house.

You bring the cheese
and I'll fetch the mouse.

You salt the ice
and I'll crank the cream.

11

Let's put our heads together

and dream the same dream.

I'll drive the truck
if you'll fight the fire.

I'll plunk the keys
     if you'll be the choir.

I'll find the ball
    if you'll call the team.

Let's put our heads together

and dream the same dream.

You dig for water
and I'll make a pail.

I'll paint the boat
   if you'll set the sail.

You catch the fish
and I'll catch the stream!

Let's put our heads together

28

and dream the same dream.

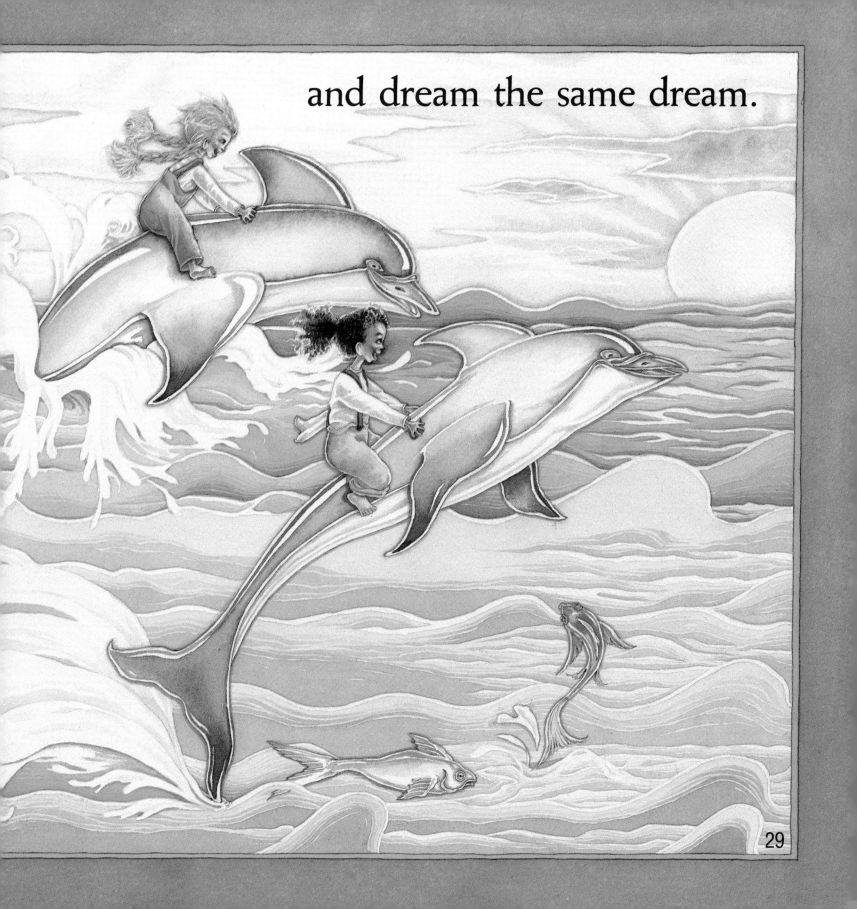

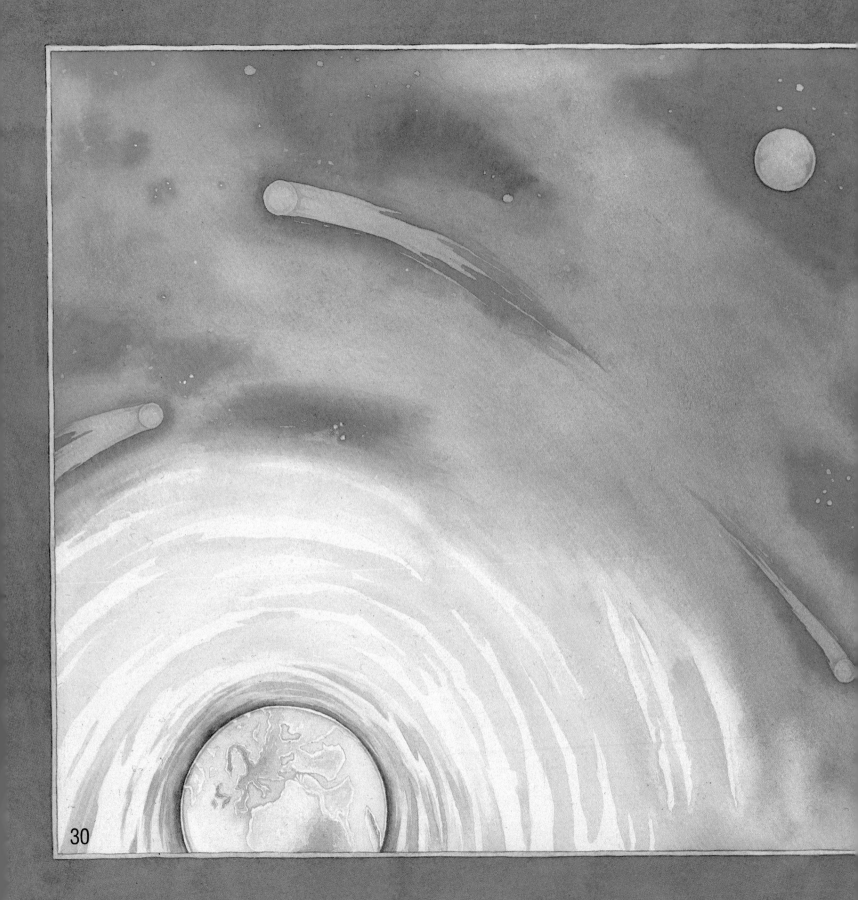